HELL'S UNVEILING

LAURA SOLOMON

Woven Words Publishers OPC Pvt. Ltd.

Registered Office:

Vill: Raipur, P.O: Raipur Paschimbar,

Dist: Purba Midnapore, Pin: 721401,

West Bengal, India.

www.wovenwordspublishers.in

Email: editor@wovenwordspublishers.in

First published by Woven Words Publishers OPC Pvt. Ltd., 2018

ANTHOLOGY

ISBN 13: 978-93-86897-29-9

ISBN 10: 9386897296

Price: $ 6 USD/ ₹ 150 INR

Printed and bound in India

Hell's Unveiling

On earth, it seemed that peace reigned at Angel's Café and foster home for troubled children located in Wellington, New Zealand. In hell, the devil was plotting. An electrical fault would do nicely he figured. He would aim for maximum chaos. The chosen wire ran behind Daniel's bedroom.

One fateful evening the devil told one of his minions to take the form of a rat and chew through the plastic coating on the wire. It began to spark. A small conflagration began and soon grew into a larger flame. Thirteen year old Daniel was asleep in his bed. The fire inside the wall gathered force and flames crept into the room where Daniel lay sleeping, flickering around his head. His room was the middle bedroom and the walls were covered with skating posters. The room was messy, with clothes strewn every which way. He did not wake up – he was in a deep slumber, dreaming of white rabbits with crosses for eyes. He began to dream he was in a sauna with the heat slowly being cranked up to maximum. He tossed and turned in his bed and pushed the blankets off with his feet. Starting to sweat, he woke up, thinking he needed a drink of water. It was then he noticed the flames that were blocking his exit, leaping across the doorway, brilliant tongues of orange. He grabbed his skateboard and wrapped a blanket around himself to protect his skin from the flames. His next thought was to help Sally who he thought might be in danger. Everybody was overly protective of Sally because she seemed so vulnerable; if she was in danger she couldn't cry out because she was mute – to everybody except Marsha that is. Or so most people thought. The

5

others had all got out and were waiting outside under a pine tree. Sally was a heavy sleeper and she might not wake in the case of a fire. He plunged through the flame and it burnt him badly, singeing the skin on his legs and torso. He still kept going to get to Sally's room. Scooping her up, blankets and all, he helped her, stumbling, down the stairs, his skin stinging. He placed Sally, who was starting to panic, under the pine tree with the others and told her to stay put, then raced back to wake Marsha. Luckily, pregnant Sheila had woken at the first whiff of smoke and got herself out safely.

Marsha, who had been dreaming of rats with devil's horns, awoke with a start and, when told of what had happened, ran to get the fire extinguisher from the kitchen. She turned the white foam on the flame to quench it and it went out. She could still see fire beyond so she ran to call the fire brigade. They raced to the scene and doused the rest of the flame. Marsha raced to Daniel's side to check the extent of his injuries.

"Don't fuss," said Daniel, who didn't want anybody making a scene.

"I'll call an ambulance," Marsha announced.

"Don't be melodramatic", Daniel countered. "I'll be fine. I'm not badly burnt. I've escaped relatively unscathed."

"You're such a good boy," Marsha said to Daniel. "Thank God for you. You've saved us."

Marsha walked across to the pine tree to check that the other children were okay. They were badly shaken but unharmed. Marsha gave a sigh of relief.

"I'm so glad you're all okay", she declared.

Marsha then turned her attention to the house. She surveyed the damage. Two entire walls would have to be replaced – the wall between Daniel's room and Sally's room and his room and the hallway. Luckily the house was insured and it would still be able to be lived in while it was being repaired.

Angel's Café was located in a beautiful old two storey building in Wellington. It featured polished wooden floors and a curved wooden staircase with a lovely carved balustrade. The outside was painted cream with apricot trim around the edges and the interior was painted pale lavender. It was a six bedroom building; large enough for Marsha to take in a number of foster children. Marsha was the motherly type and liked to fuss and coo over her charges. In the event of a fire the place could have gone up like tinder and it was very fortunate that the house had been saved. The tables were round. It was not only Marsha's house of residence, it was also her place of business and it meant the world to her. The café was located at the front of the building, facing the street. There was a large counter, with a menu board to the right listing the day's specials. Two beautiful magnolias bloomed in the garden outside surrounded by native ferns. There was also a garden of iceberg roses and lavender and another garden filled with freesias, daffodils, bluebells and jonquils. There was an old fashioned till, with a handle at the side. From the counter they served angel cakes, friands and blueberry muffins, crème brulee and cheesecakes. For breakfast there was eggs benedict, eggs on toast, bacon and eggs, and pancakes and maple syrup.

For lunch they served meals like salmon fishcakes, Marsha Lee's special cheeseburger, fried chicken burger with purple slaw and jalepano aoli, grilled fish sandwish with cucumber pickle and venison sausages with mash and Sally's homemade relish. They also opened six days a week for dinner and served fish of the day with new potates and fresh green beans, rib eye steak with chunky fries and wild rocket salad, Hawke's Bay lamb rump with spring greens, free range spatchcock, new potatoes, caraway, sauerkraut with orange and dates and finally ravioli with Sally's homemade ricotta, spinach, mushroom and garlic. For dessert they served Marsha's tiramisu, Sally's blueberry cheesecake with walnut crust, and a citron cake with lemon icing. They did a roaring trade. Marsha would stay up late into the night balancing the books, keeping herself awake by drinking numerous cups of black coffee. She did not believe in looking back in life, she was a positive thinking, having lost two family members she had been forced to be, and she never once regretted opening the lovely Angel's Café, which was open to the public six days a week.

***

Marsha filled out her insurance claim online. She had no way of knowing that the devil had planted more than one of his minions in the insurance company. The company sent a female insurance assessor to the house to take photos and to document Marsha's version of events. She carried a black satchel with a white inverted pentagram on it. Marsha did not like the assessor who she noticed sprayed themselves with a perfume called Sulphur. The assessor told Marsha that she wanted to view Daniel's room alone and that Marsha could not accompany her inside.

Three weeks later Marsha was called in to talk to the head of the insurance company. She fixed her hair in place, applied her lipstick and dressed in her best outfit but she could not control the butterflies in her stomach. She felt guilty though she knew she had done nothing wrong. It was the way the assessor had made her feel.

Two men sat laughing together as Marsha walked into the office, stopping abruptly as she entered. They gave her the once over. Not even getting up, the man on the left held out his hand for Marsha to shake.

"Hello I'm Gordon Latimer, CEO of Inferno Insurance – a pertinent name with your case. And this is Timothy Simpson, the company lawyer."

He laughed at his own joke.

"Please, take a pew."

He gestured towards an empty chair. Marsha sat down, trying not to feel like she was in the principal's office.

"So," she said. "What did you want to talk to me about?"

"Before we begin, tell us Marsha, what do you do for a living?"

"I run a foster home called Marsha Lee's Home for Emerging Angel's."

"Oh," said the CEO as the lawyer took notes, "so you run a house for delinquents, do you?"

"Look," said Marsha. "Can we get to the point please."

"It's about your case. There seem to be a few inconsistencies in the version of events that you have presented to us."

"I've told nothing but the truth so I don't know what you're talking about."

Gordon took out a manila folder full of photographs from his briefcase and laid them one by one in front of Marsha. The first photo that Marsha saw was a shot of under the bed in Daniel's room – a bottle of lighter fluid, a lighter and some matches. The next snap was of *The Arsonist Magazine* published by Burning House Press, lying on the floor near the end of Daniel's bed. The third and final photo was a shot of the single 'The Roof is on Fire' inside his CD player.

"Daniel doesn't own this junk," said Marsha, springing to his defense. "I vacuumed his room at the start of the week and there was nothing like this in there."

"Well these are the photos that the insurance assessor that we sent to your house took."

"I knew there was something fishy about her," said Marsha. "I should have followed her into the room. This evidence has been planted. I'm the victim of a setup."

"I suggest you take this seriously. Fraud is a jailable offense that could also carry a hefty financial penalty."

He tapped his teeth with his pen.

"However, we can make this all seem like a bad dream. Yes, we can make it all go away if you agree to one thing."

"And what would that be?" asked Marsha.

"We ask only that you turn your charges over to us for safekeeping. They will be well cared for at the Unhallowed Halls Home For Healthy Humans or U quadruple H as we like to call it. Yes, give us the kids and we can sweep this whole sordid affair under the carpet."

"No way," exclaimed Marsha. "I'm not letting those kids out of my sight. They're precious to me. God only knows what you'd do to them."

"Don't be so silly. We wouldn't touch a hair on their heads. They'd be perfectly safe with us."

"What do you want them for anyway?"

"We want to....to train them."

"Train them for what exactly?"

"That's our business. They will be well looked after. Fed the finest food, they will sleep on sheets of Egyptian cotton and bathe in lavender scented waters. They will dream only sweet dreams. No nightmares shall taint their slumber."

Somehow Marsha didn't find this terribly reassuring. In fact, she felt decidedly uneasy and looked around for the nearest door, hoping to beat a hasty retreat.

"Look," she said. "Let's wrap this up, let's cut to the chase. Can we sort this out here, or shall I bring my lawyer in to talk to you?"

"Oh," mocked Gordon. "Getting all threatening now are we. Just you be careful how you proceed, missy, least the whole thing blow up in your face."

Marsha had had enough. She rose to her feet and stormed from the room, slamming the door behind her.

***

Two weeks later Marsha received a letter in the mail, summoning Daniel to court. She was furious. She had thought that the men were just full of bluster and that the charges would be dropped – she had not thought that they would proceed with anything serious. However, it seemed that they meant business. Marsha walked down the hallway to Daniel's bedroom. He was sitting on the end of his bed with his head in his hands, looking down in the dumps. Given that she could sense his despondent mood, Marsha was loathe to break the bad news to him, but she knew that he would have to tell him sooner or later. She took a deep breath and said "Daniel, I've something important to tell you."

He didn't look up.

"Yeah, what gives," he mumbled.

"You're a suspect in an arson case. You need to take this seriously. It's to do with the burning down of this place. You're to appear in court in five days time. You'll need to make yourself look smart. You won't be able to wear your baggy skating clothes. I will come with you and support you. Hopefully the two of us can successfully face the adversary together because I believe in your innocence. I believe they planted the evidence, they

12

framed you and they are making you into a scapegoat. It's not okay. They are evil men. We can't let them win."

"Evil sounds right. I didn't start no fire. I might be naughty but I ain't *that* bad. I would never do anything to harm Angel's Café. This place is a home to me, a haven, the only home I've ever known. I'll go to court and tell the truth. The judge will have to believe me, he'll see the honesty in my eyes."

"Okay we'll go together, let's go shopping for some smart clothes."

Marsha rang legal aid and chose a smart young lawyer named Elizabeth Saunders who she thought would be best able to represent Daniel. Elizabeth had graduated from law school four years previously, and was hungry for action.

The big day rolled around. Daniel was so nervous he vomited in the morning and Marsha had to make him a drink of lemon and ginger to soothe his stomach. On the morning of the case, Marsha received a phone call at home saying that Elizabeth had come down with a bad bout of vomiting diarrhea. They were appointed a lawyer from the public pool. His name was Ramsay Rutledge and he had a fat stomach and carried his briefcase hanging open with papers falling out of it, unprofessionally. Needless to say, he did not create a good first impression. He did nothing to calm Daniel's frayed nerves.

"How can we win with a loser like that on our case?" Daniel hissed to Marsha.

"Shhh, he'll hear you," said Marsha in a low voice. "We don't want to put him off his game."

Marsha and Daniel walked into the courtroom with their lawyer. Once inside they saw Gordon and Timothy greasing up to the judge.

Timothy dominated the courtroom proceedings with his hotshot legal terminology. Ramsay could hardly get a word in and Marsha and Daniel could tell he seemed afraid of Timothy and what he was capable of. In the end the jury only took half an hour to decide that Daniel was guilty of arson, and although it was hopelessly unfair and unjust that was what the court had decided. Daniel was sentenced to one year in a juvenile detention centre in Wellington. The judge also stated that Daniel was a danger to Marsha's other foster children so he would not be allowed back to live with Marsha ever. Marsha held back her tears – she did not want Timothy and Gordon to see her in a state of weakness. She wanted to stay strong for Daniel.

Once she had returned home, Marsha allowed herself to burst into tears. She buried her head in the pillow in her bedroom and sobbed at the thought of Daniel, whom she had tried so hard to save, being wrenched away from her bosom and back into the cruel, cold world. A juvenile detention centre! What could be crueler? For his part, Daniel had gone very quiet, withdrawn into some distant corner of himself, where nobody could reach him or hurt him. He walked in through the doors of the house and went straight to his room, buried himself underneath the duvet and would not come out for two days. Marsha had to take his meals in to him and even then he just picked at them and barely seemed to eat.

Two weeks later Daniel had to pack his bags in preparation for the detention centre. Marsha had received a pamphlet in the post informing her that she could visit once per week only. She had vision of talking to her son through a pane of glass like in prison movies. Daniel got into the passenger seat of the car, Marsha hopped into the driver's side and they drove silently to the juvenile detention facility. Once there they had to fill out some forms and then Daniel was shown to his room which he had to share with another boy called Rig. Rig was six four and built like a tank. The first thing he asked Daniel was "So, do you play rugby?" When Daniel replied "No, I skate" Rig refused to talk to him for a month.

Marsha drove slowly home, hoping that Daniel would be okay. Upon her arrival at Angel's Café she was pleasantly surprised to find that Sally had whipped up a big batch of cream cheese and chocolate muffins. Marsha was starving and she ate two.

The devil was pleased with the outcome.

The Arrival

Sheila was eight months pregnant. Marsha distracted herself from Daniel's problems by helping Sheila prepare for the birth. They painted up an old spare room at the back of the villa to use as the nursery. They knew in advance that she was having a girl so they purchased some girl's clothes from the op shop and from Gap and found a basinet on Trade Me. Sheila was very much looking forward to the birth, which she intended to have at home, at Angel's Café. She was all prepared. She had informed the midwife of her intentions.

The day of the birth dawned bright and clear. The devil had special plans for the birth.

He would send a minion in the guise of an ambulance driver to drive Sheila to the hospital. Of course, she would never arrive at the hospital. Instead he would take her to his training centre, drop her down in his elevator shaft to hell, whereafter he would own both her and the baby. It was the perfect plan. He sent a demon named Paimon. Paimon teleported to earth, stole an ambulance driver's uniform and ambulance from Bowen Hospital and made his way to Marsha's house.

Sheila went into labour in the early hours of the morning. The midwife was called and arrived bearing Enthnox and Pethidine and a big smile. The ambulance pulled up in the driveway and tooted twice. Marsha went out to see who it was. She didn't recall calling an ambulance. The driver rolled down the window. Marsha moved across to speak to the driver.

"I've come to drive you to the hospital love", said the driver.

"Can I ride in the back with Sheila?" she asked.

"No hospital policy doesn't allow that. You need to follow a safe distance in your car."

Marsha's suspicions were aroused. She sent the driver away, telling him that they had decided upon a home birth, and home birth was what they had. The birth was easy, the baby wanted to be in this world and came out head first, almost smiling, and then with a gurgle and a kick, the umbilical cord was snipped and she was given to her mother to hold. In hell, the devil was furious. Bloody Marsha! She always got in the way. Sheila snuggled the baby in close and kissed its button nose. She named her Daniella in honour of Daniel who had now departed from the household. Daniella was a great sleeper and feeder so things went smoothly for Sheila who had only just turned sixteen. Motherhood came easily for her, she was a natural and Marsha didn't have to help much at all.

Marsha went to visit Daniel once a week. She took photos of Daniella to show him. He was mostly silent and appeared depressed and uninterested in any conversation that Marsha tried to start with him.

It crushed Marsha to see him like this but she persisted with her weekly visits each time looking to see the spark in Daniel's eyes that was once there. She hoped her visits would provide a lifeline for him and that he would not get too depressed and attempt to take his own life which she feared he might do.

There wasn't much to do in juvvie; just some boring trade classes and English, Science and Maths lessons that Daniel never attended. There was a run down basketball court. Sometimes he would shoot a few desultory baskets. There was no skate ramp. He wasn't interested in much about the centre. There was a doctor they could see if they had a medical problem and a dentist visited once every two months. There was a strong emphasis on good mental health with 'Like Minds, Like Mine' posters pinned to the wall, as if they were in a psychiatric asylum. There was a time out room, painted lavender to calm down its unlucky inhabitant, with a small pane of shatterproof glass set into the door for others to peer through, staring in at the animal trapped inside its cage.

Marsha lay awake one night and came up with a plan. She would appeal Daniel's case, pay for a better lawyer and take it to the Court of Appeal. She wasn't going to sit back and watch him go down.

The next day Marsha went to visit Daniel and told him of her plan. For the first time since he had gone in there Marsha saw some hope in his eyes.

"Is there really a chance you can get me out of here?"

"Yes, there is a good chance, you were wrongly imprisoned - it's just because the opposition had that know it all lawyer but I'm going to get a better lawyer and get you out; you will be free."

"I'll love you forever Marsha if you can do that, you don't know what it's like being cooped up in this place, I feel like a caged chicken."

"I promise I'll do my best Daniel, please be a little patient."

***

She was told to go and see a woman named Abagail Watson located at 108 Lambton Quay. Abagail was a partner at Watson and Dwight and was very highly thought of within the firm.

The word was that she won 85% of all her cases. After Ramsay's performance, Marsha liked the idea of having a hotshot on her side.

Marsha arrived at the address and took an elevator to the tenth floor. She entered a very posh reception area - the firm's name was in embossed in glossy writing upon the wall. There was also a security guard and two receptionists that looked like they had stepped out of Vogue magazine.

A designer vase stood in one corner sprouting giant fresh lilies. Marsha tried hard not to feel intimidated by the reception area. She was there on business and had as much right to be there as anyone else.

She walked up to the reception area and asked to see Abagail Watson.

"One moment please bear with me. Who may I say is calling?" replied the receptionist who donned an important looking headset upon her perfectly coiffured hair.

Marsha said her name.

The receptionist pushed some digits on her keyboard and rang through to Abagail.

"There is a Marsha Henry here to see you."

Abagail emerged after five minutes from behind the double oak doors. She was dressed professionally in a pin striped skirt suit and a nice expensive looking pair of heels. She reached out a hand to shake Marsha's and said "Hello I'm Abagail Nighingale". Something in the firm handshake and tone of voice made Marsha feel a sense of trust. She senses Abagail's goodness, her humanity. Daniel was in the right hands here.

Marsha followed Abagail back through the double doors. They proceeded down a corridor and into Abagail's office. Abagail took a seat behind a glass desk and gestured for Marsha to sit down on the other side. Marsha sat.

"Right. How can I be of assistance?" spoke Abagail in a firm voice.

"I've come about my foster son Daniel," said Marsha, pulling out a file of court notes. "He was wrongly framed in an arson case, now he's languishing in a detention centre and I want him to be set free. We only lost our case because the other team had such a hot-shot lawyer and our own was so shoddy. With someone like you on our side, I really believe we can take the case to the Court of Appeal and win."

"I'll do all I can to help," said Abagail and Marsha heaved a sigh of relief. "Let's start by you giving me a run down of the case, then I'll have a look through the court notes in my own time."

Marsha ran Abagail through the night of the fire, to the encounter with Gordon and Timothy at Inferno Insurance's headquarters. She went on to describe the court case and Daniel's sentence, then described a typical visit to see Daniel at the juvenile detention centre.

"Timothy at Inferno Insurance. Would that be Timothy Simpson?" questioned Abagail.

"Yes."

"Oh, I've heard of him, he's really ruthless, no wonder you didn't fare well."

"Yes he ate us alive. It wasn't pretty. Daniel's the one that had to suffer."

"Well, let's see if we can get him out. Leave these court notes with me, I'll read through them over the next few days and get back to you."

***

Marsha tried hard not to think about Daniel's case until Abagail rang. She distracted herself with household tasks, the baby, and helping Sally with her cooking. The phone call came two weeks after she had been to see Abagail. Abagail apologized for the delay but said she had been doing some research into the case. She stated that as it turned out the insurance assessor who had supposedly taken the photo of the arsonist's kit in Daniel's room had been caught planting evidence in the past and had been fined for it, and did not have proper assessing qualifications.

"We can get them on this point," she assured Marsha. "Don't worry, Daniel will soon have his freedom back."

Looming in the background of Marsha's mind was the question of where Daniel would live once he was free. The judge had ruled that he was not allowed to live with her so she would have to find him some other safe home. The following day she went to an adoption agency in central Wellington and tried to pick a suitable family. Of course, they wanted to meet Daniel first. Marsha simply said that he was busy; she did not mention that he was stuck in juvvie, knowing this fact would put families off. Eventually she found a family called the Robertsons, who she thought might be suitable. The best part was that Marsha already knew and liked them from one of the many Wellington foster family evenings she had attended. They lived in Kilburne and seemed like respectable citizens. The father worked in real estate and the mother was a housewife. She would be able to give Daniel the attention he craved. Marsha rung up the juvenile detention centre and explained the situation asking if she could take Daniel out for an afternoon to meet his new family. To her surprise, the centre agreed. The following Monday Marsha picked up Daniel in her car and took him to meet the Robertsons, counselling him to be on his best behavior. Daniel behaved immaculately and did not mention he was in juvvie and the Robertsons agreed to take him in as a foster child with a view to adoption at some unspecified point in the future. As a matter of fact, the Robertsons knew that Daniel had been in juvvie but they thought that he had been framed and that the situation was awful. They wanted to do anything they could do to help. Yes, Marsha had found Daniel a good, kind, understanding family. Now, all Marsha had to do was secure his freedom.

Down in hell, the Devil was plotting with his minions. Word had reached his ears that his insurance assessor had been caught out and he was not happy about it. He called a meeting of the minions, of whom the insurance assessor was one. His flunkies gathered around.

"You," he said, pointing to the insurance assessor who was cowering in the corner. "How could you let this happen. You've really slipped up."

"I…I'm sorry," she stuttered nervously. "But you've sent me on these impossible missions, I was bound to be caught out."

"Don't you dare blame me," hollered the Devil, raising one pointy, scaly finger and turning her into a pile of ash.

The other minions quivered, thinking they could meet the same fate. The devil singled out another minion.

"You, I want you to go to the juvenile detention centre disguised as a delinquent boy and encourage Daniel to escape. That will get him in more trouble."

The minion nodded obediently. The minions always obeyed their boss and now they knew not to chat back.

Back on earth Daniel was feeling cooped up and frustrated. There was no way for him to vent his copious amounts of energy. He felt trapped. The centre was very hard on the boys. They had to do chores all day and they were locked in their rooms after seven at night. They had pointless counselling sessions with dowdy counsellors who were just going through the motions. They would tell Daniel he could not heal until he had confessed to his crime, but there was no way Daniel was going to admit to something he did not do. Abagail set an appeal date at the court and Daniel was informed of the date.

Daniel had no friends at the centre until a mysterious person called Adam showed up and began showering him with attention. Daniel was flattered, he finally had a friend – the other boys had their own groups and he felt like the eternal outsider. Now at last he had his own companion, somebody to laugh with, somebody to talk to. Adam was fun and full of ideas. They asked to be roommates so Daniel could get away from Rig. This request was approved.

One night as they were lying in their bunks Adam said "You know, I can figure out how to get us out of this place. I've been in here before. Escaping wouldn't be so difficult. Let's do it! Let's make a jail break. Let's blow this joint."

"We can't do that, we'll get caught. I want to play by the rules. I don't want any more trouble."

"Oh don't be such a goody two shoes. Life was made for living. What kind of an existence is it stuck in here? We're rotting. Life is passing us by."

The night was getting late and Daniel drifted off to sleep with thoughts of breaking free drifting through his mind. In the morning he had fresh perspective on the matter and had come to the conclusion he would quite like to escape. He broke this news to Adam and it was well received.

"Great then, let's go tonight. We'll wait until the sun goes down, then we'll sneak out the back way by the kitchen and out across the courtyard. I've got wire cutters to snip through the barbed wire at the top of the fence."

"How did you smuggle those in here?"

Adam winked.

"I have my ways and means."

The day seemed to take forever to pass, but eventually it was over and Adam and Daniel snuck out the exit by the kitchen and scuttled along in the shadows of the buildings to the edge of the wall. They began to scale the wall until they reached the barbed wire at the top, then Adam cut through with the wire cutters, bending the wire back on itself. They both climbed through the gap in the wire and slid down the other side of the fence until they reached the ground.

"We're free!" said Adam, giving Daniel a high five.

Daniel danced a small jig of happiness. A dog began to bark. The sound came from the direction of the detention centre. Adam and Daniel looked at each other and then began to run.

It wasn't long before two security guards came running after them. Daniel and Adam sprinted a short distance and then scaled a nearby tree and tried to hide in amongst its branches. The security guards did not see them in the tree. They were safe. Eventually the security guards gave up searching and headed back to the detention centre. Daniel and Adam were unsure of where to go but Daniel said it was okay and they could go to Angel's Café. They headed in that direction and when they arrived they were greeted warmly by Marsha who was over the moon to see Daniel back. However, she was worried he would be in trouble with the detention centre.

"You need to ring the detention centre and tell them you have escaped. This could affect your appeal. We were in the process of setting you free legally."

Adam interjected.

"No," he said. "You can't do that! I'll be in big trouble with my boss, Satan!"

His hand flew quickly to his mouth as if he had let slip a secret. Suddenly, there was a crackle of light and Adam had been turned to a pile of ash. Marsha and Daniel stood in shock. Marsha said, 'This is the Devil's work', with a look of realization on her face.

They phoned up Abagail and told her what had happened. Abagail promptly telephoned the detention centre and informed them Daniel was going to live with his new foster family, the Robertsons. She also told them she had information that incriminated the insurance assessor and Daniel had been framed. Since Abagail was so highly regarded in the community and in legal circles they did not argue with her.

The appeal went smoothly. All accusations were squashed and Daniel got monetary compensation. He settled in well at the Robertsons, bonding with their teenage daughter and helping Mrs Robertson about the house.

***

In hell, the devil was raging.

"Why are my minions so useless! They always stuff things up! You can't get the staff these days."

He began throwing bolts of fire in every direction. His minions scattered.

"I won't be defeated. I'm coming up with a plan for earthly domination that won't fail."

The devil fired all his minions and hired a fresh batch. It was time for a change. He would train up this lot to prey on people's weaknesses and fears. They would travel to planet earth and subtly feed people negative thoughts with the aim of driving them towards mental illness and suicide. He gathered his new team of minions around him and gave them their brief.

"Our mission is to feed people exaggerated versions of their own negative thoughts. This will require you to tune into their thinking by spying on their conversations. You will need to build up a profile of what they are feeling insecure about. You will then prey on their fears. This will need to be done very carefully as we cannot fail this time. I've learned now that destruction should be slow and subtle, not instant gratification."

The minions nodded obediently.

Sheila was targeted first. She was feeling insecure about her body because she had just had a baby. The minion Zorba zeroed in on this insecurity and taunted her. First she sidled up in a centre for young mothers that Sheila attended on a regular basis, and kindled a friendship, then she slowly planted the seed. Zorba had a perfect figure, immaculate make-up, wonderful clothes and was a terrible show-off. Sheila was dressed in tatty old duds and looked like she had just rolled out of bed. She tried to make Sheila think she understood how tough it was being a young solo Mum. She tried to appear empathetic. This lasted for about a month. They began having cappuccinos and Caesar salads together at lunch time and then Zorba started in with the barbed comments.

"Looking a bit podgy round the middle today," said Zorba to poor Sheila one day.

"Oh gosh am I? That's no good. I'll have to see to that."

Six weeks into the friendship Zorba hit her with the zinger "You'll be a rubbish mother, you should have the baby adopted out."

Sheila nearly burst into tears. Although the baby was still in her womb she loved it dearly and could not bear the thought of parting with it.

"I've noticed your clothes are a lot tighter these days, you're squishing into those skirts."

"O help. Is it that bad?"

Within no time at all Zorba had given Sheila a complex and an eating disorder. Sheila began starving herself and would sometimes pass out from lack of food. She was determined to get down to the size she had been before the baby. Sheila knew she was damaging her body but she did not care. All she wanted was to be thin. She would look at herself in a mirror and all she could see was a gigantic stomach bulging out the front and a big bum hanging out the back. She hated her own reflection. The day finally came when Sheila once again fitted the clothes she had worn before her pregnancy but she still wasn't satisfied. Now that she had started on the treadmill she could not stop. She had become a perfectionist. She wanted to be thinner still. It was an obsession now. Things got dangerous. At night she could feel her heart beating loudly in her chest, struggling for life. There seemed to be no way out and no one to turn to. She was trapped in a spiral of negative thinking. Marsha noticed what was happening and grew worried about Sheila.

Daniel was approached by Semi, another of the devil's workers, who Daniel met at the skate park one Saturday. He sidled up and started talking about skating, then casually dropped a hint that he knew Dan had been in the juvenile detention centre.

"I'd watch my back if I were you," he said, with a hint of malice in his voice. "You never know when they might come for you again. You never know what they might try and frame you for next time. Might be something more serious, like say…murder."

He cackled. Daniel gulped.

"It was as if he could read my thoughts," Daniel said to Mrs Robertson afterwards. "He mentioned my biggest fear right off the bat. It was spooky. I dread going back to juvvy."

"Don't let him unnerve you," said Mrs Roberston. "After all, he's just a stranger, you don't even know him. Anybody can say something like that. Some people get their kicks freaking other people out."

Daniel was not reassured.

"You don't know what it was like in there. The place was a hell hole. I still have nightmares about it."

Mrs Robertson leaned over and rubbed Daniel's back.

"There, there. You're safe now here with me. I won't let them take you again."

Sally saw the ad in the paper.

Creative cookery with Celia Cookson. Ph. 04 616 2976.

She checked with Marsha if it was okay for her to do the course, then asked Marsha to ring up and book for her. She was accepted onto the course. She showed up the following Saturday, ready to learn. The first dish they were making was a coffee-crème brulee – the recipe provided by Celia. The dish was complicated, but Sally concentrated hard and her dessert was a great success. After the cooking had been completed, and when they were packing up to head home, a minion named Zara approached Sally.

"Congratulations on such a fine performance in the kitchen," she said enthusiastically. "I've got something to make your crème brulee even better."

She reached into her pocket and produced a small vial containing a clear liquid.

"This special French syrup will make your brulee a hit. It will bring out their hidden flavor and appeal instantly to all taste buds. This syrup will make you and your cooking famous throughout New Zealand and then the world!"

Zara slipped the vial into Sally's backpack with a smile.

Sally smiled but said nothing. Sally headed home. The following morning she was dying to try out Celia's crème brulee recipe at Angel's Café. She would serve the dessert, topped with the new syrup, to the customers. She couldn't wait to see the satisfied faces, the looks of delight. She made a phenomenal amount – forty-two desserts in total, which had sold out by the end of the day. Her vial was empty; she had distributed its contents evenly over the desserts. At the end of the day she fell into bed exhausted and happy.

The next day the phone at Angel's café began ringing non-stop. Sally thought that people might be calling in to complement her on her cooking, but from the look on Marsha's face that was not the case. Sally listened in from a position upon the stairs.

"Oh, I'm very sorry. Oh that does sound terrible. Yes of course we will give you your money back and a free coffee. Are you sure it was the brulee and not something else you'd eaten? Oh okay I see."

Call after call was the same.

"You've been vomiting all night? Oh dear, you poor thing. Come in and we'll give you a refund and a free coffee."

Marsha rung off after the last call and summoned Sally to one side. "Sally, about those crème brulee...."

Sally looked around to make sure they weren't overheard. There was no way she wanted anybody other than Marsha knowing that she wasn't a true mute.

"Yes?"

"It appears they have made people sick. Whose recipe were you using?"

"Just Celia's."

"Were the ingredients fresh?"

"Yes."

"You didn't put anything funny in them?"

"Well, I did use this fancy new syrup a friend I met on the course gave me."

"Syrup? What syrup?"

"It's special. From France. She said it would make my cooking magnificent and make me famous throughout New Zealand and then the world. I couldn't resist the potion's promises."

"Oh Sally. Somebody's played you for a fool. Let me see the bottle."

Sally handed over the vial. Marsha gave it a sniff.

"Hmm, my bet is this is some kind of poison. This is the work of the devil, mark my words. He's been stepping up his game around my charges lately. I'll have to sit you all down and have a word so you're wise as to his ways and don't get fooled again."

Health and safety got on their case, threatening to shut them down. Sally and Marsha raced around getting rid of the rest of the crème brulees. Sally became reluctant to cook, and began to doubt her abilities. She had to be carefully coaxed back into the kitchen by a clever Marsha who tried to boost her failing self esteem with sensibly chosen words. She persuaded Sally to make a batch of her fabulous Angel cakes in order to make her confident again and to have some faith in herself.

A week later Marsha gathered her adopted family together in the dining room at Angel's Café.

"Now I want you to listen carefully," she said. "Because what I am about to tell you is important. The devil is at work in your lives and you need to guard carefully against him."

She turned to face Sheila.

"Sheila, I don't know who has been convincing you that you are fat, but you have a lovely figure. You don't need to lose any more weight. You're fine just as you are. You need to learn to love yourself."

Sheila burst into tears.

Daniel had been especially invited over to Marsha's for this talk.

"And Dan. Don't worry about being sent back to juvvy. You're going back there over my dead body. I'll do all I can to keep you out. You haven't done anything wrong, so there's no need to have a guilty conscience."

"Sally. Don't accept random 'gifts' from strangers. You never know what you might be getting yourself into. Not everybody has your best interests at heart. You don't need to add to your talents because they're fine. You don't need special potions to make your food taste beautiful and win fame and fortune."

"For some reason, Satan is honing in on us at the moment and we can't let him in when he comes knocking, with all his wiles and temptations. I believe he has underlings he sends to planet earth to do his dirty work for him, and it's these demons that have been appearing in your lives. Devils in disguise. Cunning. They intend to cut you down. Undermine you. They don't want to see you proud and strong, they want to see you cowering, crumbled in the corner. The best thing to do is to ignore them, come home and tell me. I have ways of dealing with them."

Marsha retired briefly to the kitchen to fix coffee and a plate of Sally's berry muffins as refreshments. She hoped she hadn't given too much of a lecture, but she wanted her team to be wise to the devil and his ways, otherwise they would fall victim to his game plan.

Marsha attended faithfully attended church every Sunday. She took the children with her. She sang along to the hymns and followed the passages as they were read from the bible. Her love of God was devoted and true. She got down on her knees and prayed every night for the things she believed in. She prayed for health and harmonious living for her children, for peace to reign at Angel's Café and for steady custom. She did not pray for another husband to come along; she did not dream of replacing Don. He had been a good husband; nobody could fill his shoes.

Down in hell, the devil began scheming. He had been beaming up footage of Marsha counselling her team and he did not like it. She was thwarting his plans. Marsha was strong, stronger than he had thought. He needed a way to take her out, to take her down. He thought for a bit and then decided there was nothing else for it – he would have to visit earth himself, in disguise, gain her trust and then screw her over big time. Sell her down the river. He would go disguised as a social worker, somebody Marsha would not suspect of having evil intentions. He took three young minions to one side and briefed them.

"Now I know you all lack experience but I am trusting you with an important mission. You are young and I don't know how competent you are but I am relying on you not to muck this up. You are to come with me to Wellington, where you will go disguised as foster children and penetrate the innermost depths of Marsha's sanctuary. I will be the social worker who presents you to her. She is soft-hearted at her core, so I feel she will take you in. Once inside you are to play up and generally wreak havok and make her life a misery. This will hopefully have the effect of making her doubt her capability as a foster mother. I want her to stop believing in herself. I want to thwart all her plans."

The minions nodded obediently, pleased to have been trusted with a mission. It got boring hanging around down in hell. There wasn't that much to do, once you had washed your hands in the same sulphuric geyser fifty times.

Dennis D'Uville

Dennis D'Uville took a small apartment with the teenage minions in central Wellington one Monday. He did not have many belongings, just a folder of fake credentials. The owner of the apartments noted he traveled light. Dennis was tall and lean, with a pointy nose and long, thin fingers, the nails of which were filed into sharp points. His hair was black and glossy and his eyes were a piercing shade of sea green.

The morning after settling into his apartment Dennis telephoned Marsha and introduced himself as the new social worker in town. He said he was employed by the government. Marsha thought this was perfect timing as she could use some help dealing with the kids who lived with her and their new problems. Dennis said he had some new people for Marsha to meet and that he hoped she could take a few more people into her home.

The following day Dennis showed up with a portfolio of photographs of children and their written profiles. First up was Jim Scott, who according to his written statement was into needlecraft. Jim hailed from the Wellington area and was looking for somewhere stable to live, a good home environment. He was seventeen years old and, judging by his photo, reasonably handsome. Next on the list was Richard who said his favourite sport was boxing. He claimed to love animals and had always wanted to live on a farm. The final person was Dahlia who said she was a collector of beautiful items. Dahlia also claimed to be handy with a sewing machine and said she could sew whoever adopted her outfits.

Marsha said she would take all three. Although this would make Angel's Café somewhat crowded, she said she would make room.

"I understand you've got room in your house at the moment", said Dennis. "One of your lads has moved on hasn't he? Look," he continued, "I've got these three kids I desperately need to place."

Dennis said he could help Marsha sort out the problems she was having with her adopted family. Marsha said those words were music to her ears. Dennis said he had wrestled with many demons in his time, but he tried not to let them get the better of him. He smiled, though it was more like a grimace.

"Are you taking the children to church", asked the devil with a wicked gleam in his eye.

Marsha said she was - she took them every Sunday.

The first meeting between the demons and the children was in Angel's Café. Marsha did the introductions and told them all that Sally did not speak. Sally served them friands and angel cakes with cream and yoghurt. Jim, who was very greedy, ate three friands and two muffins. The demons and Marsha's existing foster children all got along together fine and there were no fights or personality clashes which was a miracle in itself. It was decided that Daniel and Jim would share a room and that everybody else would have a room of their own as it was a six bedroom house.

Within the space of a week the new charges had demonstrated their naughty behavior much to Marsha's chagrin. Marsha asked Richard to take charge of the garden, taking up where Daniel had left off. Unfortunately, he put her best blessed salt around the plants, killing them, pulled up all the plants when he was supposed to be only ripping up weeds, and generally wrecks the garden. Marsha had been given a silver birch by Daniel. It was still young. Richard ripped the branches off to play at sword fighting with Jim, leaping around the garden yelling 'Look at me, I'm King Arthur', showing off to an invisible audience. The kids made the baby cry, boiled over the pots on the stove, ate all of the food from the fridge, didn't put things away and told Marsha they had done their chores when they had not done them. Dennis was forever popping in and out of the house, checking up on progress. He always leapt in fright at the sight of one of the crosses or bottles of holy water that were dotted about the house thought Marsha never witnessed this.

Jim got high on P one night and was talking to Dahlia in front of Sally about how they have been briefed by the devil. The minions had made the foolish assumption that Sally was stupid because she was mute. Of course, Sally ran and told Marsha what she had heard. Marsha's suspicions were aroused. Maybe this Dennis was a suspicious and evil character. There was no doubt that the kids were very naughty. She decided to confront Dennis. She took her best cross from where it lay carefully wrapped in tissue paper and hung it around her neck to give her strength. She cornered Dennis one evening and told him his number was up. She didn't want him, with all his negativity, hanging around anymore.

"Marsha, I have met my match with you," said the devil. "I know now you are touched by God. I want you to know I wasn't always one of the wretched. As everybody knows, I used to dwell in heavenly realms, I was an angel, the angel of light. They called me Morning Star, Lucifer light bringer. The angel of the abyss. It's true I suffered something of a fall from grace, but let's not go there."

"I knew it," said Marsha, pointing a finger. "You're the devil himself come to visit me. Dennis D'Uville indeed! Surely you could have disguised yourself better than that. Get away from me you evil spirit. I banish you back to hell!"

She took the cross from around her neck and held it out in front of her. White light blazed from her eyeballs and struck Dennis in the chest. He began to squirm and change shape, melting away under Marsha's force. Golden light emanated from the cross and lit up the room. The devil winced and covered his eyes, moving to cower in the corner.

"That's it, you wimp," scoffed Marsha. "Run and hide in the corner, like the weakling you are. Stay away from my family, I don't want you preying on them, their vulnerabilities. Feeding off their fear. Now get your arse back to hell where you belong!"

There was a puff of smoke and the devil was gone, just a smouldering pile of sulpur left where he had been. Marsha got a brush and shovel and cleaned up the mess. When she went through to find the 'children' he had burdenered her with she found they too had vanished and she realised they must have been his helpers, fresh from

40

the infernal realms. No wonder they had been so naughty; he had been coaching them and egging them on behind the scenes.

Unhallowed Halls Home for Healthy Humans

The devil was furious his plan had not worked out. Furious and humiliated. The minions he had taken with him to earth had been watching the scene with Marsha from the doorway and now they were laughing at him, mocking him behind his back. No respect, that was the problem. He resolved to concentrate on the UHHHH or U quadruple H – otherwise known as the Unhallowed Halls Home for Healthy Humans. This area was to be a training ground for minions; this was where he would train people up to be his slaves. It was a large complex; in the centre of the main hall was an elevator shaft. After the completion of their training, on 'Graduation Day', graduates were dropped down the elevator shaft straight to hell, where they were to serve the devil forever more as minions. They would have no free will; they would exist as extensions of the devil's will. They would do his bidding, carry out his evil plans. People would be lured to the UHHHH thinking they had won some special job offer and this was their training. He would find them on the streets, on buses and trains and over the internet. Humans were gullible; they would be sucked in. The devil was arrogant – he thought all humans were stupid.

The UHHHH was situated in an abandoned warehouse on the outskirts of Wellington. The devil resolved to do a recruitment drive. He would target victims via email, fliers and pamphlets. Yes, UHHHH would be full – packed to the rafters with minions in training. David became one of those minions. He was nineteen and had spent two years in a juvenile detention centre. When he was let out he was homeless and that was when he had been recruited. The devil preyed on the vulnerable. David had come across one of the devil's fliers blowing loose in the street. *Special job offer, free training, accommodation and meals contact 04 690 8666. Don't delay, call today to take advantage of this marvelous opportunity. Be quick, limited spaces.* David only had a few coins in his pocket but he used one of them in the nearest payphone. He dialed the number and was directed to one of the devil's minions.

"Hello, how can I help you?" spoke the minion into the phone.

"Hello, my name's David, I came across one of your fliers. I was wondering what the job offer entails."

"It's a special deal," came the reply. "Free training and accommodation and a lucrative job at the end of it."

"Okay, where do I go to train?"

"You need to go to the Unhallowed Halls Home for Healthy Humans or U quadruple H as we call it. You'll find us located on Aurora Terrace. Don't tell anyone where you're going."

David jumped at the offer. Being homeless sucked. Here was a golden opportunity that had fallen into his lap – he'd be a fool to turn his nose up at it. He made his way to the address he had been given. The complex was a huge and forbidding building, towering high above all the other dwellings in the area. David was a little intimidated by its exterior, but he gathered his courage and made his way inside. The interior was created from concrete and steel. He was greeted by a man who wore a name badge labelled

Abaddon and said "Welcome to the Pleasuredome. Could you please hand over your ID? I've got a few forms for you to sign. Follow me to the office please."

David obediently followed Abaddon to the office. Once there he handed over his ID and signed the requisite forms. The forms stated he had to do whatever he was instructed, that no cellphones or communication with the outside world was allowed, but in return he would be well looked after, receiving free food and accommodation for no upfront fee. There were boxes to tick denoting skills and abilities. David ticked the box for martial arts, as he had trained in this in the past. He also checked the computer skills box, as he had learned this at high school.

He was also handed course materials and told to swot up. David looked over the material. It all seemed very strange, but he had signed up for the duration and he intended to stay the course. The courses all had strange names such as Kitten Killing 101, Deception 203, Martial arts 304, Shape-shifting 205 and computer hacking 206. David couldn't make much sense of it but he played along. Abaddon threw him a uniform – a black tracksuit with a red inverted pentagram on it. Later in the dormitory, David tried the uniform on for size. It was a bit baggy around the bum, but it would have to do.

"Come on" said Abaddon. "I'll give you a tour."

David took a deep breath and said, "Okay then."

They started at one end of the building at the gym. A few possessed looking people were working out on the machines. Everyone looked so fit and muscly, David felt daunted, thinking his body could never become this toned.

"I suggest you start working out in the gym," said Abaddon. "There'll be fitness tests to be passed. We don't only train the body. We also train the mind. We aim to produce ninjas."

"I have to tell you I'm homeless. I don't think I could ever be a ninja."

"That's the first step. We teach you to believe in yourself. Here we teach you to become confident like soldiers. No doubt, no fear. No looking back at where you came from. Here you can invent a new persona, a brand new you. We even give you a new name at the end of the course. How does that sound?"

"That sounds great," enthused David. "I've always wanted to reinvent myself."

Next Abaddon took him to view the dormitory. It was painted forest green with thin mattresses and army blankets on the beds.

"This is the male's dorm," said Abaddon. "No entry into the female dorm is allowed."

After this David was shown the kitchen, dining hall and café. In the café there was an enticing range of sweet treats, pastries and muffins with cream cheese icing on display.

"Gosh," said David. "Looks like somebody's trying to fatten us up."

"Oh it won't pay to get too podgy here," commented Abaddon. "You're in training to become a ninja remember. However, we have to feed you well so you've got the energy to fight. I don't agree with these sweet treats, but I must say I do like a good roast from time to time. Alcohol, cigarettes, all drugs and sexual relations are strictly banned on sentence of death. On the plus side, I promise you your dream job at the end of all this training."

"Death!"

"Yes, death. We don't muck about here."

"But isn't that illegal."

"We make our own rules here. You'll learn that with time. Our motto is Obedience to Him."

"Him? Who's him?"

Abaddon tapped the side of his nose with one finger.

"Our leader who you'll meet in good time."

David was a bit mystified by all this but he didn't like to ask to many questions as he sensed Abaddon's air of impatience. He was grateful to have a roof over his head and delicious food to eat and he decided to keep his mouth shut.

"Now it's time to show you our crowning glory – where you'll go on Graduation Day."

He headed for the centre of the building and David followed in his wake. In the middle of the great hall stood a glass elevator which had been decorated up with fairy lights, tinsel, glitter balls, and a large sign which read *Congratulations! Destiny Awaits.*

"What's that?" asked David.

"That's the elevator. Where you go on Graduation Day," said Abaddon, when you finish all your courses and training. You'll be taken back to the outside world where your dream job awaits you."

"Sounds fantastic. I love the way you've decorated it up."

"And that's the end of the tour," said Abaddon. "If you'd like to go back to your room and study up on the course materials that would be most helpful."

"I'll do that," said David.

Back in his room, David took out the course materials, once again mystified by the strange topics. He opened the first book of readings, Deception, and began to read.

To become a skilled ninja you will first have to master the art of deception. Humans are stupid and easily fooled. However, don't let any of these giveaway signs trip you up!

1) *Pause or delay. Make sure your responses to the person's questions are immediate and smoothly delivered.*
2) *Do not attempt to cover your mouth or eyes. This is an obvious sign you are lying.*
3) *Do not clear your throat or swallow too often.*
4) *Do not raise your hands to your face too often.*
5) *Do not groom yourself.*
6) *Do not babble. Excessive talking is a certain signal to your victim you are not telling the truth.*

David put the book down and picked up another, Kitten Killing 101.

The purpose of this class is to eradicate all the feelings that won't serve you in your new job such as remorse, guilt, sympathy and empathy. The aim of the exercise is to kill as many kittens as it takes for all traces of these traits to be eradicated from your brain. Throughout this procedure you will be hooked up to an EEG which will monitor your brain waves. You will not be able to pass this course and complete this section of the training until you have successfully rid yourself of these unhelpful and limiting emotions.

**Kittens are supplied by Pets 'R Us who have no knowledge of their fate.

David shuddered and closed the book. Kitten killing! What kind of place was this. Maybe he'd wag that class he thought to himself.

David picked up the next book. *Shapeshifting* was the title.

"This will be interesting," he thought to himself.

He'd heard about shapeshifting and thought it sounded cool. He'd like to be able to change into a giant, or a sphinx. He turned to the first page.

Shapeshifting is a question of mind over matter. You will learn to envision transforming into the creature you wish to become. Most of our transmutations are human to animal. People change into rabbits, alligators, leopards, rats and the most common, wolves. You'll find changing back the most difficult element of the equation as part of

48

your metamorphosis will involve losing your own mind and taking the mind of another living being. Some people have become trapped in their morphed form forever.

David shuddered. He couldn't imagine being trapped for eternity in the form of a rabbit or a rat. That seemed a terrible fate. Perhaps he could skip shape-shifting too, he thought to himself, although he knew in his heart if he missed too many classes they would kick him out and he would be back on the street, back fending for himself, amongst the junkies and the misfits. He gave himself a stern talking to.

"David," he said. "You have come here to learn. This place can also provide you with a temporary sanctuary, a home. They're also promising you a dream job at the end of it and Lord knows your job prospects weren't looking crash hot before you came here. Be grateful to have a roof over your head and three square meals a day."

David gave thanks to whatever deity might be listening for sending the flier advertising this marvelous training complex his way. That had been a fortuitous twist of fate.

A bell rang. Checking his watch, David saw it was 6pm. Assuming the bell signaled dinner time, he made his way down to the dining hall and found it packed full with other trainees, many of them new recruits, judging from the way they were looking around awkwardly, not quite sure of what to do. David watched as somebody who must have been here a little longer walked confidently up to the buffet, filled her plate and sat down at one of the long tables to eat, sprinkling her meal with salt and pepper, topped off with a dollop of relish. He followed suit and sat down next to the girl. They did not make eye contact. They did, however, strike up a conversation, initiated by the girl.

"So, been here long then, or are you a newbie?" she asked when David sat down.

"I'm just new here," said David. "What can you tell me about the place?"

"Well you'll want to keep your wits about you. Our boss can be pretty frightening, especially when he loses his temper, which is often. He keeps us all on our toes. One false move and its out with the cattle prod."

"A cattle prod! Not really, you're pulling my leg."

"No I'm not. He gives us electric shocks if we step out of line. He runs a tight ship. Better stay in top shape, both mentally and physically around here. He likes discipline and order. Rigid. Army style. You'd have noticed that theme coming through in the dorm."

"Sounds terrifying."

"You'll get used to it. People can get used to anything given time."

"Sorry, what did you say your name was?"

"Cynthia."

"Hi Cynthia, I'm David."

"Hi David, it's nice to meet you."

"What about the lessons? What do you think of the lessons?"

"The boss says they're good for us. Teaching us what we need to know. To become ninjas. Or whatever. I'm not sure I buy into everything he says. I'm too cynical and hard bitten. What about you?"

"I didn't like the sound of the kitten killing much. I thought I might skip that class."

"O no, you'll be out the door if you do that. The boss doesn't take kindly to people cutting class. You might surprise yourself. When I did it, the first five kittens were difficult, painful to kill, but after that it was easy, I just ignored their meows and kept strangling."

"Sounds brutal."

"The boss wants to kill all kind feelings in us."

"But why?"

Cynthia shrugged.

"It's part of his agenda. He wants us to become machines. Sub-human. I found the shape-shifting class most interesting. Most people chose lycanthropy and became boring old wolves. Snore. Me, I decided to become a panda and they gave me a shoot of bamboo to chew on. I have always loved pandas so it was a pleasure to become one."

"Now that's more up my alley."

By this time Cynthia had finished her meal, and she gathered up her empty dinner tray and utensils and said 'Well, I'll probably see you round', then walked away, depositing her tray, knife and fork on a trolley which had been placed near the doorway for that purpose.

David rose from the table, pondering the conversation he'd had with Cynthia. She hadn't complained too much about being in this place, in fact, she seemed to quite like it. David decided to retire to bed, suddenly feeling tired and overwhelmed by the day's events. He had been given two pairs of pjyamas that had the same strange symbol as the tracksuit – the inverted pentagram. David fell asleep almost immediately, into a deep slumber dreaming of zombie kittens and shape-shifting ninjas. In the morning there was a bell, and a voice came over the loudspeaker, summoning them to the breakfast hall. David looked at his clock. It was only 5am – he wasn't used to getting up at this hour. He took a leisurely shower then strolled down to the breakfast hall. He was greeted by a sea of angry faces as he entered through the swinging doors. Abaddon was up the front of the hall with a microphone. When he saw David he said, "David, I see you finally decided to join us. So glad you could make it."

David sheepishly slid into the nearest chair.

"Stand up boy!," instructed Abaddon.

Obediently, David stood.

"Could somebody please tell our latecomer the rules," said Abaddon. "You really should have read it in the literature I gave you. Lester, can you tell David the rules."

A tall red-head stood up and smugly said "Everyone must be in the dining hall within ten minutes of the siren. This

52

is punishable by demerit points. Yes, we run a points system here. Everyone starts off with one hundred and now you've just lost twenty."

David slumped back into his chair, red-faced and embarrassed. Abaddon began his morning greeting, by saying "Repeat after me, *I pledge allegiance to the unhallowed halls for healthy humans. I devote my body, mind and soul to the master.*"

David looked around as everyone repeated the chant loudly and proudly, thinking to himself he'd better make sure he did not slip up again. He wanted to find Cynthia later and ask her about the points system and what happened when you got to zero demerit points. He vowed to himself he'd read all the literature he'd been given so he didn't stuff up again.

After four weeks of being at the complex, David was slowly but surely becoming more and more brain-washed. His soul was transforming and he was losing any goodness that had been in him. It had only taken four kittens before he had lost his remorse. He excelled in the martial arts class and got a thrill in learning computer hacking. He'd mastered the art of shape shifting quicker than expected and received As in all his classes. He lost no more demerit points in his time there as he found out from Cynthia that getting down to zero meant death. He kept to himself and he kept his mind focused on finishing the year and acquiring his dream job with the generous salary he had been promised.

After six months David had become unrecognizable to those who had known him before. The training had made him ruthless and barbaric and he would kill at will. Two days before graduation day, a nervous tension ran through the graduates. They were excited but also apprehensive as they knew they'd be leaving the safety of the complex never to return. Pamphlets were handed out containing instructions on how to prepare for graduation day.

Wear your best clothes. Polish your shoes to a shine. Impeccable grooming is required. You will be meeting your boss very soon and you want to make a good impression for the next leg of your journey.

David and three others were scheduled to enter the elevator at twelve noon. That morning a banquet was put on – turkey with cranberry sauce, deep-fried camembert cheese, lamingtons with sweetened whipped cream, and a steamed pudding rich with raisins. When noon rolled around David, Cynthia and three others were led into the great hall by Abaddon and escorted towards the elevator. The doors of the elevator opened and they stepped inside. As the doors closed behind him, David noted Abaddon's malicious grin, signaling something was amiss. He suddenly got a sense he'd been lied to and played for a fool. He got a jolt as the elevator moved as he was expecting it to go up, but instead it descended rapidly downwards.

"Hey," he said. "Where are we going? What's going on?"

"I dunno," said one of the other graduates. "Maybe it's faulty. I thought we were meant to be going up."

Before they knew it the elevator stopped. One of them touched the door and then recoiled due to the heat. There came a scratching from the other side of the door, the sound of nails on steel. Nobody moved to open the doors. It was dark and David could not see two inches in front of his face. Finally the doors opened and there stood a creature with seven heads, long pointy fingernails and a tail which ended in a sharp point. One of the girls screamed and David's mouth fell open in shock. It clicked in his mind what was going on. He found himself looking out at a barren landscape of steaming hot concrete broken up by the odd geyser. Small flames flickered in the distance. He stared at the creature before his eyes. So this was the 'Him' they were all talking about. One of the graduates fainted and the man with seven heads demonstrated his power by turning her to a pile of ash.

"We can't afford to have any weak fainting types down here," he said with a sneer. "Let that be a lesson to the rest of you. Any sign of weakness and you'll be turned to ash."

David quivered. Cynthia piped up.

"Where the hell are we?"

"In the bowels of hell, sweetheart. And you're the best looking minion I've ever been sent. What did you say your name was again?"

"I didn't say. But it's Cynthia."

"I like your attitude. I like a lady with a bit of sass."

He winked. Now it was Cynthia's turn to shudder. This monster with seven heads had a crush on her! God could this day get any worse. The devil began a speech.

"Friends! In case you are wondering who I am, I am Beelzebub, Satan Himself, the Grand Master, He Who Must Be Obeyed."

He wore a long purple cloak and he strutted around with it like a model on a catwalk, vainly preening himself, flexing his horns, twirling his tail and admiring himself in the mirrors which were placed strategically to either side of him.

"God what a show-off," said Cynthia.

"I heard that," hissed the Devil, with his snake-like tongue. "Don't be getting *too* sassy or you'll meet the same fate as your friend."

"Your year at the complex was to prepare you for your descent to hell. You are now my slaves. You have sold your souls to me. You no longer have free will. You will do what you are told until the end of time. You will do my bidding, you will do as I desire. As minions you will receive new names." He gestured toward the first two graduates. "You can become Amon and Bile." He looked at Cynthia. "Coyote – that will do for you sassy lady." He pointed one scaly finger at David. "And you, you can become Dracula. Right no mucking around. I'm going to assign you your first task. My motto is to lie, steal and destroy wherever possible. Your mission will be to travel to the earth's surface. To gain control of the earth we need to divide and conquer. Your first task will be to tempt drug addicts who are trying to quit into taking drugs again. I will give you a supply of what they crave and you will leave it lying around their flats and houses, right under their noses. You will be implicit in their downfall. You will also tempt men to partake in domestic violence by telling them lies about their spouses such as that their women have been cheating on them, stealing their money or tipping their booze out."

He held up a jar with some sort of fungus in it.

"This is Diplodia Stalk Rot. Perfect for destroying corn crops. I want some of you to land in the Heartland of the United States and release this fungus. That should put paid to a few farmers' dreams and cause despair and poverty. I feed off those. Dracula and Coyote, you can go together on the drug mission. You'll find everything you need on the display table to my right – the cocaine, the heroin, the speed. Don't sample the wares yourselves. Amon and Bile you can take the corn. Be sure to spread the fungus far and wide and smear it properly into the corn. We want to destroy as many hopes and dreams as possible."

Dracula and Coyote picked up the drugs. Amon and Bile took the fungus in a jar from Satan.

"Prepare yourselves to be teleported," said Satan with a twitch of his tail. "Please close your eyes for this part of the procedure."

The four graduates closed their eyes. Soon they were feeling a warm wind rushing past their ears and they felt a spinning sensation. Amon and Bile opened their eyes to find themselves in the middle of a golden cornfield that seemed as if it stretched on forever. They took the fungus from the jar and, walking down the row, smeared it on corn intermittently, on one in every twenty stalks. They progressed through five rows this way and at the end of it congratulated themselves on a job well done.

Dracula and Coyote were greeted by a vision of a London junkie's messy flat. Porn magazines were strewn across the floor, along with needles and old junk food wrappers – Crisps, MallowPuffs, McDonalds wrappers and old bottles of alcohol.

"Christ what a mess," said Coyote. "Somebody needs to clean up this place. Be careful not to step on any of those needles Dracula."

Dracula stepped carefully across the floor, taking out a bag of speed and positioning it on the makeshift coffee table that was just an upside down beer crate. Coyote dropped her bag of cocaine on the kitchen bench amongst the fly-ridden weeks old dirty dishes. A mouse scurried across the bench. They found the junkie in the bedroom passed out so they put a pouch of heroin in his outstretched hand. Following this they moved on to a housing estate located nearby.

The estate was made of brick with a large cracked concrete forecourt with a washing line stretched across it. Two African boys played rounders on the forecourt. Seeing one of them had left his bag on the sideline, Coyote slipped a bag of cocaine into it.

"Wait until his mother finds that!" said Dracula.

They headed into the centre of the estate. African music drifted down from the top floor. A lady was out sweeping her balcony. Cigarette butts floated down to the ground as she swept. Coyote and Dracula crept in through a door that had been left ajar and found themselves inside a tidy flat, oddly decorated with taxidermied animals. Two teenage African boys sat on the sofa, passing a joint back and forth between themselves. They were oblivious to Dracula and Coyote who carefully slipped little packets of methamphetamine into the inside pocket of a black leather jacket which was hanging over the back of the sofa. Then they quietly retreated and made themselves invisible. It was time to report back to the devil.

Dracula took out his mobile phone, texted 666 and got through to Satan himself.

"Calling home, mission accomplished," read the text.

The next minute they were being beamed back to hell, experiencing the same sensation of wind rushing past their ears and spinning as if in a vortex.

In hell, the devil was fuming.

"This latest batch of humans aren't getting the hang of the shape-shifting. Are they mentally retarded or something?! I haven't got the patience for this. They'll be cast into purgatory!"

He paced back and forth. Two flickering forms appeared, riddled with static, then became solid entities before Dracula's very eyes. It was Amon and Bile, fresh from their corn mission, reporting back to base. Another successful operation.

Cynthia stood in the corner with her leg tucked up against the wall behind her. The devil began eyeing her up.

"It's not often I see pretty ladies like you standing around," he said suggestively.

"Don't be disgusting," replied Cynthia. "I wouldn't fall for a man with seven heads. Which one would I kiss."

"Don't be fooled by appearances. Aren't you at least a little intrigued about what it's like to date a man with multiple heads?"

"Can't be any worse than the dickhead I've been out with."

"So you're willing to take a chance then? How do you fancy a drive in movie?"

"Do they really have movie theatres in hell? I didn't realise that."

"Is that a yes then?"

"A tentative one I suppose."

So it was that Cynthia and the devil found themselves on a hot date the following Friday. The devil drove a Chevrolet, which he parked at an angle in front of the big screen. The movie screening was The Void and both Cynthia and the Devil became engrossed in the action. Partway through the movie, the devil slipped his arm around Cynthia and began to caress her shoulder. The devil's arm was warm and Cynthia could feel the heat coming through his fingers. It felt comforting. She reached up her own hand and stroked his fingers. The devil moved in to kiss her with two of his heads, lips pouting. His lips found hers and his serpent-like tongue slid down her throat. Cynthia began to choke and pushed him away.

"No tongue please," she said with a grimace.

The devil had many faces and he showed only some of them to Cynthia. The devil showed her his pleasant face with the aim of getting her into bed and hid his shadowy faces. Despite herself, Cynthia was sucked in and she found herself falling for the devil's charms. When he invited her back to his bedroom she did not refuse. The bed was covered in red satin sheets and the duvet cover had a roaring tiger imprinted on it. The prince of darkness was a perfect gentleman under the covers. His seven heads came in handy. He used a condom. He knew, although Cynthia did not that his seed was superhuman and would shoot straight through the latex. He satisfied all Cynthia's needs and in the morning made her a freshly brewed cup of coffee.

"Thank you for a lovely evening," said Cynthia politely. "We must do it again sometime."

Later, she shook herself, hardly believing she had actually had sex with the devil. Would she become pregnant to him? Give birth to a demonic baby with multiple heads? She could hardly fathom this reality, but she had not been using any contraception, so she knew she might have to face it sometime if she did not take the morning after pill. Cynthia did not make it to a pharmacy in time to get the morning after pill. The devil telephoned her that afternoon and told her he was in love and he could fulfill her heart's desire if she would only give up her earthly existence and dwell in the infernal regions with him

61

forever. Cynthia was reeling from the night before and her head was in a muddle. She told the devil she needed some time to sort herself out and get herself thinking straight and she couldn't make any firm commitments at that stage.

One Saturday a customer came to the café wanting to paste a flier advertising a special training complex on the outskirts of town. Marsha took an interest.

"What's this new complex then?" she asked.

"It's a training ground where you learn to become a ninja and train for your dream job."

Something about the flier aroused Marsha's suspicions. Perhaps it was the white inverted pentagram in the lower left hand corner or perhaps it was the phone number *04 690 8666.*

She decided to investigate further. She would go to this training ground herself and find out what it was all about.

The following Friday Marsha dressed in a simple skirt and blouse and headed to the training complex. On arrival she was greeted by Abaddon who gave her the same tour he had given David. He also handed her the course materials which David had acquired. Marsha took in her surroundings which were concrete and steel, but what really caught her eye was the glass elevator which seemed out of place.

She felt like an undercover agent. Marsha took the elevator and descended into hell. She spotted him standing against the far wall. He had seven heads and they looked in seven different directions. When he poked out his tongue she could see it was forked like a snake's. She knew she had come face to face with Satan himself, Beelzebub, the Devil. She would play him at his own game, she would take him down. Marsha gripped the handle of her sword tightly. She stood six paces away from the devil and pointed the sword in his direction. Then she lunged at him. The devil did not flinch. The sword plunged into his chest. He was impaled. A thin wailing sound escaped the devil's lips. Then he withered. Slowly but surely he faded away. Marsha congratulated herself. She had won this war. The war against evil. A war for all time.

"That was too easy", she thought to herself. Further, the devil had died with a slight smile on his lips and a knowing glint in his eye. Although Marsha was ignorant of the fact, the devil knew that he had fathered a son and therefore that his evilness would not die but would be passed on.

A lightening bolt of energy circled the earth.

Once the devil had been taken down Marsha wasn't quite sure what to do with herself. What was she doing in hell anyway? She decided to head back to earth to see what had been going on up there. She stepped inside the glass elevator and headed towards earth. The elevator took her at the speed of light towards the earth's crust. Once she had reached the surface of the earth Marsha stepped out of the elevator and onto the busy street.

Back on planet earth there were ramifications to Marsha slaying the devil. The crime rate improved in several countries and people and countries that used to be enemies started to support each other in a unified way. People of the world became one nation, united together with no more separation. Golden light beamed through the clouds overhead, prisons were shut down due to lack of offenders, hospitals were closed through lack of sickness, and a nuclear disarmament program took place on both sides of the Atlantic. Peace reigned on planet earth.

Cynthia took the elevator back to earth to resume life there. Six weeks after sleeping with the devil Cynthia realized she may be pregnant and went and bought a pregnancy test. To her horror the strip in the centre turned pink. A baby was growing in her womb! Cynthia didn't know how she felt. The night she had spent with the devil had been marvelous, but she had refused his further advances as she had thought he was too fast and dangerous. She had put distance between them and not pursued the relationship. She hadn't heard from him since that fateful night. Now she was pregnant with his baby. Cynthia picked up the phone, dialed 666 and tried to get hold of him. One of his flunkies answered the phone.

"Hello is Satan there please?" asked Cynthia politely.

"Who him? No, didn't you hear the news. He got stabbed through the heart by some holy bitch who came on a special crusade to kill him. She succeeded too. He's six foot under pushing up daisies, love. Sorry to be the one to break the terrible news. I hope you two weren't close."

Cynthia hung up the phone feeling stunned. The devil was dead? Now what? She was up the duff and destined to become a solo Mum, living off a stingy benefit and eeking out a miserable existence. At least the devil would have been able to keep her in luxury and finery. With him she would have dined on the finest trout, sipped the richest wine and scoffed the most decadent chocolates. He knew how to treat a lady. Should she have an abortion? She knew she'd have to make a decision soon.

When she was two months pregnant, Cynthia got out *Rosemary's Baby* from United Video and the next day Cynthia made an appointment at the Te Mahoe Abortion Unit. There were protesters outside on the day she rolled up to the clinic and Cynthia felt a pang of guilt when she saw their placards. She pushed past them brusquely and made her way inside. Unbeknownst to her, the devil had sent one of his minions disguised as an abortionist, and although he pretended to perform an abortion, Cynthia left the clinic with the baby intact. The pregnancy continued.

The baby grew, and kicked and slammed its fists into her ribs and she wondered whether the baby would take after her or its father. What would its temperament be? She got a lot of heartburn, she had terrible morning sickness. The devil had shown her his sweet side, but she had also seen him reduce a human to a pile of ash. Would this baby too possess this dubious skill? How would it get through life in one piece if it had multiple heads? It would be teased, picked on, reduced to tears and be forced to run away and join the circus.

All Cynthia's fears were alleviated the day she gave birth to a single headed child with perfect eyes and nose. It looked up at her and cooed and Cynthia fell in love. It had the devil's eyes, sea green with flecks of blue. He poked out his tongue and she saw it was forked. She continued to love him anyway. She named him Balaam. He had pale skin which made him look anemic; you could see the veins pulsating through it. He had a cry like a wailing banshee. Cynthia clutched him protectively to her chest and swore to guard him from the dangers of the world. He looked so small and vulnerable, it was hard to believe who his father was. She didn't want any harm to come to him and she knew the world was a perilous place, full of hidden tricks and traps that could take a person down.

Time passed and it soon became evident Cynthia had given birth to a child prodigy. She enrolled him in Brighter Horizons kindergarten where he excelled in all areas. By the end of his first year he was reading Charlie and the Chocolate Factory to her, knew the times table off by heart, was proficient in basic algebra, and had grasped major science concepts – the solar system and its place in the universe, cognitive load and atomic science. He was a real whiz kid and Cynthia was proud of him. Despite his lineage and his early wailing, which he grew out of, he was a good natured child who grew quickly. In no time at all he was attending Brooklyn primary school where he excelled in all subjects and rapidly progressed through the system. By coincidence, it was the same school in which Sheila was to enroll Daniella.

Shortly after his seventh birthday Balaam began to light random fires. Cynthia was disturbed by this and she knew it was his infernal heritage beginning to show. Where would it lead? Was she rearing a hellraiser? He started by lighting a fire on her front porch. Cynthia returned home from her job as a real estate agent to find the flames flickering, panicked and turned the hose upon it. The porch was wooden and rickety and it wouldn't take much for it to catch alight and burn the house down. The next fire he lit was at the primary school. The food for the cafeteria was brought to the school in banana boxes and a stack of these sat outside the back door to the café. Balaam looked at the banana boxes with interest. Did he have the will power to resist setting them alight? After all, fire was intrinsic to his nature. He took out a cigarette lighter he had found one day on the way home. He was fascinated by the flickering flame. He did not know who his father was. All he knew was when he lit fires he felt a sense of security. He set the banana boxes alight. He stayed around long enough to see the flames lapping around the boxes then disappeared.

Cynthia was called to the principal's office. One of the other kids in the playground had witnessed Balaam setting the boxes alight and narked. The principal was furious and gave Balaam a stern warning. He told Cynthia they would be keeping a close eye on Balaam in future and arson would not be tolerated in the school.

Two weeks after this incident Balaam was walking home from school, when he passed a vacant lot, McGuire's Field where his interest was raised by an abandoned vehicle. The door was ajar. Balaam opened it and climbed inside. The upholstery was torn and the hessian was hanging out. Second nature took over. In the glovebox he found a stash of old newspapers. He crumpled them up into a ball and stuffed them into one of the rips. This did the trick. He lit the papers and the fire started to take hold. The car seat went up in flames with a whoosh. The smoke coming off it forced Balaam to get out of the car. Balaam ran away in fear. He'd already been in trouble with the school principal and he didn't want any more grief. As he was running away he ran straight into old Mrs Jenkins who lived at Red Beach Ave. Mrs Jenkins knew Balaam from the local Baptist church where Cynthia would take him in hope that he would not follow in his father's footsteps.

"Why don't you look where you're going young man," said Mrs Jenkins.

"Sorry," said Balaam over his shoulder and kept on running.

Mrs Jenkins was muttering under her breath as she approached McGuire's Field. As she glanced across she saw the old car well alight. She put two and two together and reminded herself to speak to Cynthia next time she saw her. In the meantime she had to ring the fire brigade. She took out her cellphone and dialed 111.

That same night, after school, a policeman came to the door of Balaam and Cynthia's house. The incident was explained to a shocked Cynthia who could see that Balaam was starting to get out of control. Cynthia was besides herself as to what to do and asked the advice of the policeman. She told them his father had been into fires and the policeman suggested counselling for the boy. Because his was underage they could not prosecute him, so they recommended he attend some youth counselling sessions run by the justice department. This would be a very fortunate turn of events as Marsha happened to be one of the key counsellors they contracted in. The counselling session was scheduled for a week later and

Cynthia took Balaam to an office space in the city to meet Marsha. The moment Cynthia and Marsha met they clicked. After the session with Balaam Marsha asked if she could have a session with Cynthia on her own. It was during that session that Cynthia blurted out she had given birth to the son of the devil.

"Oh, the father can't have been that bad."

"No I really mean it. The real devil. I did it down in hell. He seduced me."

Marsha was horrified. She was taken aback because she had killed Balaam's father. She was determined not to mention this to Cynthia.

Loki and the Orb

Now that the devil was dead, the minions took over and ran hell. They took some time to celebrate the death of their boss who most of them had secretly hated. There were celebrations in hell the night the devil died.

Loki was handsome, charming and very, very dangerous. He had been the devil's right hand man and had served with loyalty. He had briefly lamented the death of his superior, then moved quickly on. There was no point in grieving. Loki had secret designs on the top job now that there was a vacancy. Somebody would have to move in and take over. Hell needed a leader or the minions would lack direction. Chaos would reign. They needed order; a firm hand. Loki knew he was the man for the job.

He appointed his own assignment. Like his prior manager, he had designs on Marsha and considered her a major threat. She was such a goodie two shoes it was sickening; she needed to be taken down a peg or three. Loki teleported to earth disguised as a property developer named Julian Renshaw. Like Dennis D'Uville before him, he set himself up in an apartment in central Wellington. He began to frequent Angel's Café to scope out Marsha. On his fourth visit he made his move. As Marsha was pinning some notices to the community noticeboard he sidled up and pressed his shoulder up against hers.

"I've been noticing the way you move," he said. "Very graceful. You're too good for this place. Nice lady like you shouldn't have to work. You should be being constantly pampered by a sugar daddy and kept in finery."

Marsha turned to stare at the man who had spoken to her. She sniffed.

"I am a lady of independent means, thank you very much," she said huffily. "I don't need a man to take care of me. I can take care of myself."

The minion held up one hand to placate her.

"Please, I mean no offense. I only want what is best for you."

He looked directly into her eyes with his baby blues and held her gaze for ten seconds. Marsha looked quickly away. He handed her one of the business cards he'd had printed.

"I'll be back to visit you in a couple of days," he said smoothly then walked calmly away.

Despite herself, Marsha was curious. Who was this handsome stranger who had walked up to her so casually? It had been a long time since any man had shown interest in her and she had to admit to herself she was flattered. Don had died a long time ago and she had been cruelly lonely in that time. At times, life had seemed nothing more than one cruel blow after another as if some malicious god were watching from upstairs and had it in for her, determined to make her life a misery.

Julian Renshaw returned two days later, as promised. This time he looked even more handsome and Marsha found it hard not to stare at him. She told herself to stop being ridiculous and busied herself in the kitchen, whipping muffin batter and manufacturing a batch of icing. Julian stepped through the kitchen doorway and into Marsha's workspace. Marsha wasn't quite sure what to do. Should she tell him this was private space and ask him to please step back into the dining area? She didn't really want to do that. She held her breath. Julian approached and put his hand on her shoulder. Marsha felt a warm glow spread from his fingers down her shoulder and arm.

"I was wondering if you would care to join me for dinner?" said Julian.

Marsha blushed a brilliant shade of red.

"I...I....well, that would be lovely," she found herself saying.

"I'll pick you up around seven," said Julian.

True to his word, Julian was outside Angel's Café at seven. He drove a Lexus RX 350.

"Great bit of land you've got there," he said to her, when she got in the car. "I've been looking round for something similar to purchase myself."

He took her to Ortega restaurant. Marsha ordered Fresh Clevedon Pacific Oysters and Julian ordered sautéed paua with glazed pork cheek, pickled shiitake, bok choy and ginger wine dressing. Julian showed off and ordered a bottle of Tattinger Comtes de Champagne Rose 04 from Reim at a cost of $990 per bottle. Julian worked as a property developer and was not short of money. Marsha's eyes nearly popped out of her head when she saw the price listed on the menu. Julian was attentive and the conversation flowed easily. The night flew by quickly and before she knew it they were heading out the door. When Julian suggested she come back to his place for a nightcap she didn't say no. *Why not?* she thought to herself. She was having a great time. They arrived back at Julian's house and Julian fixed Marsha a gin and tonic or two. They sat together on Julian's black leather sofa and Julian leaned over and put his arm around Marsha's shoulders and began rubbing her arm. Marsha leaned in closer. He felt so warm, so comforting. Julian brought his head forward to kiss her and Marsha did not move away. One thing led to another and, Julian was so seductive and attractive that, despite being a nun and having taken a vow of chastity, Marsha soon found herself breaking those vows, and wound up in between the sheets with Julian. Julian was athletic in the sack. He was well toned and obviously worked out at the gym. He became overheated and at one point Marsha thought he was going to catch fire. When she asked him if he was okay he said "It's alright, it's just my Viagra."

Marsha was pleased with his performance and found herself happily lying in his arms afterwards. This was the first lover she'd had since Don had died and she felt satisfied and comfortable. Marsha was quietly smitten. She couldn't believe this dark handsome stranger had taken such an interest in her. Marsha was charmed by the whole experience.

They dated twice more, he took her to two different high class restaurants, wining, dining and bedding her. Marsha became giddy with the attention, feeling almost like a schoolgirl again. What was happening to her? She hadn't felt like this in years. The more she saw of him, the more he seemed to include her in his affairs, even to the point where he asked her to bear witness to one of his property contracts.

Unbeknownst to Marsha, Julian then took that signature and transposed it with the help of a photocopier onto a Sale and Purchase agreement stating Marsha signed her property over to him. Marsha was in the kitchen whipping up a lemon meringue pie when they arrived. They wore slick black suits and carried sharp looking briefcases. Marsha went to the counter to attend to them, thinking they were wanting a reservation.

One of the men turned to the other and said "This is the perfect spot for a six storey apartment block. Julian has certainly done his homework on this one, he'll make a fortune. Uncanny, isn't he. Uncanny and cunning. He could take candy from a baby."

Marsha was just about sick. An apartment block! She couldn't believe she'd been duped.

"Excuse me," she said. "May I enquire as to what you are talking about?"

"Sorry sweetheart, didn't you know. Julian's bought this place off the owner. He's going to bulldoze the café and put up an apartment block."

"But no sale took place!"

"O yes it did. Julian's got the papers. I've seen them with my own eyes. Maybe your boss didn't tell you she was selling."

"Err..excuse me…I *am* the owner. Or at least I thought I was."

How could she have been such a sucker? How could she have fallen for those baby blues? She had thought when she killed the devil that all the deceit and trickery was behind her. It seemed this was not the case. She took out her mobile and dialed his number. It was disconnected. She hung up the phone. Next she tried his developer's office. The receptionist answered.

"He's left. He didn't even give notice," she said.

It finally dawned on Marsha. Her sweet loving Julian was connected to hell. The hot sweats, the charm, now that the blinkers were off she could finally see how she had been manipulated. She had fallen for the oldest trick in the book. Just then her phone rang. It was Sheila, babbling something about Sally and Daniel.

"Slow down Sheila, just tell me what's happened."

"It's Sally and Daniel, they've been taken. Body snatched in the night. Their beds were empty this morning. Where can they have gone?"

Marsha put two and two together. Julian would be responsible for this too. That man was bad news. She had to stop him. Chances were he had disappeared with her foster children down to the bowels of hell. She'd been into the abyss once before to kill Satan himself; she could do it again. She headed back to Angel's Café and took her finest Hattori Hanzo sword from it's sheath. She would be needing this. She headed in the direction of the warehouse intent on meeting Julian again and having a show down. She had to rescue her children. She felt an exhilarating energy start to rise in her. It was the energy of anger. How *dare* he steal her children? Marsha had been very busy and had not eaten in 12 hours. She was running on adrenalin as she entered the warehouse. The elevator stood in the centre of the main hall, still decorated up with its silly *Congratulations!* sign. The doors opened and Marsha stepped inside. The doors then closed behind her and she was whisked briskly down to hell, the temperature in the elevator rising as she descended. The stench of sulphur hit her as the doors opened and the sight of two or three hundred minions milling about reached Marsha's eyes. Some of them were doing stretching exercises to keep supple, some of them were toasting marshmallows over the fires of hell, some of them were cooking what smelt like whale blubber in a gigantic cauldron. They were so preoccupied with what they were doing that the did not see Marsha sneak around the corner and into the Old Quarter, on the hunt for Julian. She overheard some of their speech.

"Hey stir the stew dumbo! Don't forget it's for his lordship Loki."

"Yea I wonder how it went for him on his mission to earth disguised as a property developer named Julian Renshaw."

"Oh, knowing him he'd pull it off. He's that bloody smooth."

She entered a dark tunnel lit by glowing candles. Passing through this she entered a cavernous area which ended in a dark lake, with a small jetty and an aluminium boat tied up. From her previous sojourns in hell, Marsha knew there was a tavern known as The Queen's Blessing located on the other side of the lake. Marsha jumped into the boat, grabbed the oars and started rowing towards the other side. The lake consisted of black tar, stank of sulphur and bubbled as she made her way across it. Several fires flickered on its surface, like angry tongues. Nobody could be seen for miles. Marsha prayed she would find Julian known in hell as Loki without having to look too much further as she was becoming awfully hungry, felt faint and her stomach was grumbling. After ten minutes rowing, she reached the other side. She stepped out of the boat and onto a surface of rough red scree. Two volcanoes could be seen in the distance – lava flows streaming down their sides. Up ahead on the left she could see the glow of the tavern lights. It seemed so welcoming, but Marsha knew in hell looks were deceiving and much evil took place within its walls. She was hoping to find Loki here. The bar was filled with minions drinking, getting drunk and hoping to get lucky with one another. Marsha was starving. The blackboard was advertising the day's special which was devilled sausages and bacon. Marsha ordered this and washed it down with Devil's Purse beer. This revived her stamina and allowed her to gather her wits and continue on with her mission.

Marsha left the tavern and followed the path which went around the lake. To her relief, she saw a familiar figure standing in the distance practicing what looked to be some form of Tai Chi. She moment she saw him, Marsha's anger returned. She drew her sword, walked up to him and pressed it to his throat.

"Just who do you think you are?" she said, fuming.

The blood drained from Loki's face and he shook with fright. He'd had his eyes closed doing Tai Chi and had not seen Marsha approaching. She had crept up softly.

"Look I can explain everything," he said. "But not here. Won't you come and see where I dwell. I'd love to show you around. I keep a lovely garden. It's not all fire and brimstone down here."

Marsha did not remove her sword from his throat.

"Look buddy, I'm not falling for your smarmy tricks anymore. You've played me for a fool once too often. *WHERE ARE MY CHILDREN?*"

"Don't worry about a thing. They're as safe as houses."

"I want to see them. Show me. I don't believe you."

"Follow me."

He set off at a brisk pace across a field of singed grass and Marsha nearly had to run to keep up. Up ahead was an elaborate forest green topiary labyrinth laid out in a square design, twisting and turning on itself in a design that was dizzying to the mind. Loki entered the entrance of the maze and disappeared around its first corner. Frightened to lose him Marsha ran behind. He wove his way deeper into the labyrinth. It was a struggle but Marsha kept up the pace, all the time with her hand gripped tightly around her sword. They approached the centre of the labyrinth, which was paved with hard orange brick. Skeletons hung from the hedges. Bones lay scattered upon the paving. One of the skeletons stepped forward and spoke.

"We are the lost ones. Won't you come and join us. We are the ones who never made it home. We starved to death."

Loki stopped and reached inside the purple cloak he had stolen from the devil after he'd died. He drew a dagger he'd kept hidden from its sheath and lunged at Marsha, successfully stabbing her in the arm and drawing blood. Marsha yelped and leapt away. Now it was Marsha's turn to prove herself. Unfortunately Loki had stabbed her in the arm with which she held her sword, so she was forced to fight with her weaker left arm. She swiped at the femoral artery in his inner thigh. Marsha hit home. Loki cried out in pain and blood began seeping through his thick canvas trousers. Then he laughed, cackling.

"Ha ha, you won't take me out that easily," he said.

Marsha didn't answer. She was starting to feel nauseous and faint from her wound. She could feel the blood seeping from the wounds and dripping from her fingers. She willed herself to continue fighting. Loki could see her start to stagger and tried to take advantage of this opportunity. He dived at her with his dagger but Marsha jumped away and he missed. Marsha stabbed her sword into Loki's solar plexus and he called her a bitch. Anger rose in Loki and he used this anger to overcome his wounds. He drew himself up to his full height and thrust the dagger into Marsha's chest, stabbing her in the heart. As he withdrew his dagger, blood poured from the wound and Marsha fell to the ground.

"It's over now," she thought to herself, her vision fading. "I'm as good as dead."

Her thoughts turned to Daniel and Sally. They would be stuck in hell forever now; doomed to dwell in the abyss for all eternity. Loki came to stand over her in triumph. He laughed at her demise.

"Not so clever now, are you nun? How could you possibly think you could win against me? You were a fool to take me on. Well, fool," he said, raising his dagger high in the air, "it's time to die."

Marsha began to pray. Silently in her mind, she longed for something to save her. Staring at Loki, looking into his blue eyes that she was once so attracted to, she saw nothing but hatred in his face. Suddenly Marsha saw a flicker of light coming from behind Loki, a swirling, pulsing round light that seemed to be travelling at a great speed towards the back of Loki's head. Marsha couldn't distinguish what this light was but she felt an overwhelming feeling of peace from its presence. As Loki was bringing his dagger down toward her throat the light which Marsha could now see was some kind of orb suddenly smacked Loki right in the back of the head. Loki's eyes widened then rolled into the back of his head as he fell sideways, unconscious.

The orb floated above Marsha emitting a luminous blue glow and making a low humming sound. It landed on her chest directly on her stab wound, healing the flesh and skin. Marsha instantly felt filled with a quiet soothing energy. She had regained her strength. Her heart was healed. She would do to him what he had done to her. She rose to her feet, stood over Loki's unconscious body and drove her sword deep into his heart.

"I have to find my children," thought Marsha to herself.

She didn't have a clue which way to turn. The orb flickered on and then off. It moved a few paces ahead of her to the right as if indicating for her to follow it. Marsha followed. It moved on, as if willing to show her the way. Marsha gave thanks to God for sending her the orb to heal and guide her.

Along they went, with the orb pulsating on and off and Marsha following in its wake. It wove its way in and out of the hedges and eventually they came to the exit of the labyrinth. Marsha followed the orb across the singed grass and through a valley lined with caves. In hell, the vast majority of the minions dwelt in these. Large portions of hell consisted of hard rock. Some of the caves were decorated with spray-painted symbols with a fire outside, one had a skull on a stick which made for a makeshift letterbox. Some minions were standing at the entrance to the cave watching Marsha nervously, as word had gotten around that she had just slain Loki. Marsha felt protected by the orb. She felt powerful and confident and on a mission to find her children. Nothing was going to deter her. The orb led her to an elaborate looking wooden dwelling with Loki written on the letterbox. Marsha sensed the kids were inside somewhere. She entered the house and walked into a large lounge area. Animal rugs were displayed upon the floor with their heads still attached, eyes staring. Pictures of Loki decorated the walls, some with candles on either side, as if he was creating a shrine to himself.

"How could I have fallen for this creep?" Marsha thought to herself. "Love definitely is blind. He must have had me under some kind of spell."

Marsha could feel her children were close. Two fires were lit in the main room and the heating was turned up to full. She entered a hallway which was also lined with pictures of him. It twisted and turned and became a stairwell. The orb hesitated at the stairwell, waiting for her. Slowly ascending the stairs, Marsha noticed the temperature rose even more as she climbed. They came to the top storey and the orb hovered in front of one of the three doors that were up there. Marsha turned the handle of the first door but it was locked. The orb then drifted through the door disappearing. Marsha looked on astonished as the door creaked ajar. Once inside Marsha immediately spotted Daniel and Sally tied with rope to a large pillar in the middle off the room, mouths gagged, eyes wide with fear.

"Darlings!" Marsha exclaimed rushing towards them tearing frantically at the rope's knots. Once the children were unbound they ripped their gags out of their mouths and hugged Marsha, crying with relief. The orb then started glowing brighter and moving towards the window with urgency. Marsha followed it to have a look what was going on outside. A crowd of minions had gathered outside the house carrying flaming torches, angry looks upon their faces.

"Water," croaked Daniel. "We've been three days without any water. We're parched."

Marsha led them to the kitchen tap, taking two glasses from the cupboard shelf. Thoughts of the minions gathered outside were at the forefront of her mind. Suddenly, a flaming rock flew through the kitchen window.

"Come on," said Marsha. "Out the back door. Run if you have the strength."

Daniel and Sally were weak as they had spent three days without water or food, but they staggered towards the back door, following Marsha's lead. The front of the house was on fire now – the crowd had been intending to burn them alive. At the rear of the house, a path led down to a small stream. The orb hovered in front of her.

"Elevator," Marsha said to it desperately. "Can you help us get back to the elevator please?"

The orb flickered off and then on three times and then began to move along, following in the rough direction of the stream. The three tired earthlings pursued it. The stream became a river, gushing in a torrent steadily onwards and Marsha, Daniel and Sally half walked, half ran along its banks, heading in what they hoped was the correct direction. Eventually Marsha saw the lamplights of the Old Quarter up ahead. The elevator shaft was around her somewhere. The orb led them successfully through the Old Quarter and directly to the elevator. Marsha blew it a kiss and once again gave thanks to God for sending her this helper.

They stepped inside the elevator and the doors slammed shut behind them. The lift began its ascent and had Marsha had never been so grateful. She was being carried away from danger and back to safety. They came out in the training complex and made their way through the hordes of minions in training, back to Angel's Café. Daniel and Sally headed straight for the kitchen; they were starving after their ordeal and Marsha had to admit she was hungry too. She hadn't eaten anything since the devilled sausages. Sally and Marsha cooked them all eggs benedict and they ate greedily, washing it down with cappuccino and orange juice. Afterwards, they retired to their respective bedrooms and everybody fell into a deep slumber.

The Children

Daniella and Balaam attended the same intermediate school – South Wellington Intermediate School. Daniella was a year ahead of Balaam, who was eleven years old. Although she was no dummy, Daniella was not in Balaam's league academically. Balaam stood head and shoulders above the rest. In a world of coal, he shone like a rough diamond. The two children were friends and helped each other through some of childhood's stormy weather such as bullying incidents in the playground (Daniella getting her hair pulled, Balaam having sand thrown into his eyes in the sandpit) and sat together at lunchtime. Together they unintentionally solved a murder case that had been left open by the police. It was the case of Julia Higgleton, a photographer from Hamner who went missing in the Otari-Wilton's Bush in the 1970s. They did not set out to look for her. One Saturday they took the No. 14 bus to the area and began exploring. They had taken a picnic lunch and intended to be there all day and ironically it had been Daniella's birthday and she had been given a camera. She wanted to take photographs of the old trees in the area. They explored in the morning and in the afternoon got a bit lost, just slightly off the beaten track, stopping for lunch in a grove of trees. They ate hard-boiled eggs, canned salmon on rye bread with lettuce and tomatoes and fresh granny smith apples. They washed it down with orange juice. As Daniella was looking at the flora something white that was sticking up out of the ground caught her eye. She called out to Balaam.

"Hey come over here and check this out!"

"What is it?" he shouted back.

"Don't know. Come and have a look."

Balaam walked over to where Daniella crouched and they both started clearing the dirt away from around the white object. As it emerged it became clear it was a bone. As taught in her biology class Daniella recognised it as a female femur.

"We'd better do the sensible thing and take it to the cops," said Daniella.

"Do we have to? I always feel like I've done something naughty when I see a policeman."

"There might be a reward," said Daniella. "This bone might be super lucky and bring us wealth and fame."

Balaam scoffed.

"Dream on," he said. "Time to get out of the clouds."

They marked the area with two sticks laid into a cross, then walked back to the main road and caught the bus into town.

The police station was located on Victoria Street. They climbed the stairs and entered through the white aluminium self-opening doors. Balaam approached the counter ahead of Daniella.

"Hello, how can I help you," spoke the lady behind the counter.

"Hi, we were exploring in Otari-Wilton's bush and we came across a buried bone. We dug it out and it looks like a female femur. We thought we'd better bring it to you."

"You've done the right thing. Can we please have look at it."

Balaam handed over the bone. It landed on the counter with a soft thud. The woman picked it up with a look of surprise.

"It does indeed look like a femur. I'll take it down to forensics for documentation and analysis. I'll also get Officer Kibble to come and take a statement from you both."

An hour later the police gave them a lift home, congratulating them on a job well done. The police said they would be in touch about the future of the case.

Two days later they received a phone call from Officer Kibble telling them they had been instrumental in solving the murder case of Julia Higgleton who had disappeared in the seventies under suspicious circumstances. He also alluded to the fact that there was a reward that was never claimed and he would discuss it with the Detective Inspector who was involved with the case to see if Daniella and Balaam were eligible to claim it.

"Told you so," said Daniella to Balaam, somewhat annoyingly.

"Yeah, yeah," replied Balaam. "We haven't got the money yet. I wouldn't get your hope up too high. Might only be a couple of bucks."

The money was paid out a month later – two thousand five hundred dollars to each person. To their dismay, both their mothers took over and told them the money would have to be invested wisely and not spent.

"Boring!" exclaimed Balaam.

Solving this case cemented their friendship, and they were bonded together even more tightly. Joined at the hip. They did everything together; attended Blue Light Discos, went on picnics at the beach and hung out together during the holidays.

One Christmas holidays Balaam, who hankered to learn how to drive (his mother would not teach him, claiming correctly he was too young) decided to steal a car and teach himself. He targeted a Ford Cortina that had been parked up along Oriental Parade for over two months without anybody moving it. He shared his plan with Daniella, thinking she would be supportive and go along with his plan. The opposite was true.

"Don't be stupid," she said. "You'll end up getting prosecuted. You're old enough to be sent to juvvy now. Are you planning on a life as a career criminal?"

"I'm not stupid enough to get caught. I'll do it in the dead of night. Sneak away after lights out, after midnight. Break into the car using an old coathanger. Seen it done on TV plenty of times. Easy. Don't try and stop me Daniella."

True to his word, Balaam waited until midnight, took an old wire coathanger from the wardrobe and then snuck out the bedroom window. It was dark except for a pale sliver of moon and the streetlamps which cast their yellow glare. It was the middle of winter, and he'd forgotten to wear his coat. He slipped, shivering, through the icy streets until he reached Oriental Parade. The car was in its usual place. He approached, twisted the wire into a helpful shape and slid it in through the window which, being an older car, was slightly loose. He hooked the wire around the lock, gave it a flick and up it came. Balaam had been reading books on hot-wiring cars, and he successfully used this technique. He got in behind the driver's wheel – his dream had come true! He bunny-hopped down Oriental Parade – he couldn't get the hang of putting the clutch in, changing gears, while slowly accelerating. The clutch was stiff and his legs were too short to reach the pedals properly. He had also forgotten to turn the lights on. Suddenly, another car had come up behind him, lights blaring in his rear vision mirror, blinding him, leaning on their horn. Balaam panicked. He couldn't get out of the way fast enough. Still looking in the rear vision mirror, Balaam kept his foot on the accelerator pedal. There was a almighty bang, followed by the chinking of metal and the sound of breaking glass. A sinking feeling hit Balaam's stomach as he realized he had hit a stationary car. Lights went on in nearby houses.

Balaam leapt from the Ford Cortina, leaving the motor running. He ran for his life down Oriental Parade, back to the perceived safety of home. He climbed into bed and pulled the covers up over his head, wishing he had listened to Daniella.

The missing wallet was discovered the next day. Balaam woke up and went to go to the corner store for a bottle of milk. He searched around for his wallet but it was nowhere to be found. Then it dawned on him. No, it couldn't be, could it? Surely God didn't hate him that much. He prayed it had not dropped out anywhere near the car he had broken into. The wallet contained a photo of himself with Daniella in it.

The wallet was found by Samuel Roberts who was out for his morning jog. Balaam had gone back to the car to try and find his lost wallet. It was gone. The jogger had it in his possession. As he was searching frantically in the Ford Cortina for the wallet, his head beneath the seats, he did not see a police car pulling up. He did not notice the policeman until he was standing right behind him. The jogger had handed the lost wallet into the policeman for safe-keeping. Balaam had a feeling he was busted.

"Well, returned to the scene of the crime, have we. Like they always do."

Balaam jumped with fright, smacking his head on the dashboard. Rubbing his head he turned to see a cop leering down at him with a stern look on his face. Balaam tried to make a run for it, but the cop was too quick and grabbed him by the arm.

"No sonny, you're coming with me. Your looks match the photo in this lost wallet. Don't know how you thought you could escape my hawk-like eye."

Balaam said nothing, knowing he was in deep trouble. The cop put him in the back of the police car and they

90

drove in silence to the police station. Balaam considered trying to jump out when they stopped at red lights but was too scared to.

Once they were at the police station, Balaam was interrogated by a senior officer who noted his name and address from the ID in his wallet.

"Been out stealing cars, I hear?" he said. "We can't have you heading down a criminal path. How old are you, son?"

"Eleven."

"Too young to be formally charged. We'll send you home to your mother and have a word with her. Let her decide what your punishment shall be."

"Do you have to tell her? Can't we sweep this one under the carpet?"

"No way. If you think you got away with it you might be tempted to do it again. Come on, follow me outside and get in the car."

Balaam dutifully followed the officer back to the same car. Once again, silence reigned in the car on the way to Cynthia's house. Balaam was too petrified to speak and the officer was obviously not the chatty type.

When they arrived at Balaam's home, they entered the brick abode via the front door and found Cynthia in the kitchen paying her bills. She looked surprised to see a policeman and said "Oh Balaam, what have you been up to now?"

The policeman explained the situation and Cynthia turned pale.

"I'm so sorry officer," she said. "He's never done anything like this before. Leave it to me. I'll handle him. He's my son."

"Is his father around?"

"No, his father…..his father's dead."

"I see. Well, good luck straightening him out and keeping him on the right path in life."

The officer left the house briskly.

Balaam was left alone with his mother, who would decide his fate. She looked at him sadly.

"Oh Balaam," she said with a sigh. "You've really let me down. I was so hoping you would not grow up to be one of those boys who gets in trouble with the law. Tell me, why did you go and steal a car?"

"It's just I so badly wanted to learn how to drive and nobody would teach me. I thought I could teach myself but I crashed the car."

"I'll teach you when you're fifteen. Just demonstrate a little patience, please."

"So – let's get it over with. What's my punishment to be?"

"You're grounded for a month. No hanging out with Daniella after school or at weekends. You're to come straight home."

Balaam pulled a face.

"And you can wipe that smarmy look off your face too, mister. You did the crime, now do the time. Now go to your room and don't show your face until dinnertime."

Balaam went to his room and sulked. Why were adults so horrible? All they did was issue instructions and tell you off when you did something wrong. Balaam couldn't wait until *he* was an adult and he could give orders of his own and have other people obey him. Alone in his room, something hardened in Balaam and he became determined not to let the world get the better of him, never to let other people get the upper hand. As for what sort of adult Balaam would become, that is a tale for another day, a story yet to be written in its own good time, an episode yet to unfold that shall make itself known in another time, in another book, another chronicle that will be laid down.

THE END

TO DO – ON days she meets devils marsha has nightmares. Dreams of falling into burning lava of volcano or being forced to take a shower in a geyser with a pitchfork pushing her in.

To DO – marsha is epitome of health and never gets sick, bugs go round but she never gets them, has to have first aid kit for kids but she never uses it.